Shawn Taylor
5-15

GO AWAY, CROWS!

GO AWAY, CROWS!
A Bantam Book

Simultaneously published in hardcover and trade paper/September 1989
"Bantam Little Rooster" is a trademark of Bantam Books.

Library of Congress Cataloging-in-Publication Data

Mason, Margo.
  Go away, crows!
  "A Bantam little rooster book."
  Summary: Big Pig and Little Pig try various methods of getting rid of the
crows that hang around their house before they are successful.
  [1. Pigs—Fiction. 2. Crows—Fiction] I. Prebenna, David, ill.
II. Title.
PZ7.M414Go   1989   [E]   88-8045
ISBN 0-553-05817-7
ISBN 0-553-34725-X (pbk.)

Published simultaneously in the United States and Canada

PRINTED IN THE UNITED STATES OF AMERICA

WAK   0 9 8 7 6 5 4 3 2 1

21432

GO AWAY, CROWS!

by Margo Mason
Pictures by David Prebenna

E
Mas

A BANTAM LITTLE ROOSTER BOOK

NEW YORK · TORONTO · LONDON · SYDNEY · AUCKLAND

Big Pig and Little Pig lived
in an old stone house.

It was a cozy house—
perfect for the two of them.

One day Big Pig heard loud noises.
Caw, caw! Caw, caw!
Big Pig frowned.
He said, "Little Pig, look at those crows.
I do not like them."

"Why not?" Little Pig asked.
"This is *our* house," Big Pig answered.
"I do not want to share it
  with a bunch of noisy crows."

But the big, black crows
liked the cozy old house.
They liked the fence.
They liked the steps.
They liked the porch.

Every day the crows came.
Every day Big Pig said,
"Go away, crows!
Go to your own house!

Get off my fence!
Get off my steps!
Get off my porch!"

Little Pig said, "I have an idea.
We can keep the crows away if...."

But Big Pig did not listen.
He had an idea of his own.

Big Pig said, "Watch me!
Watch me scare those crows."

Big Pig filled a bucket with water.
Then he threw the water out the window.

"Look!" he yelled to Little Pig.
"I scared those crows away.
I knew my idea would work!"

The crows went away.
But they came back.

Big Pig yelled,
"Go away, crows!"
This is not *your* house!
This is *my* house!
This is *my* fence!
This is *my* porch!

The crows went away.
But they came back.

Little Pig said, "I have an idea.
We can keep the crows away if…."
But Big Pig did not listen.
He said, "I have an idea of my own.
I'm smart—smarter than those crows.
Watch me write something smart."

Little Pig asked, "Are you sure
this sign will keep the crows away?"

Big Pig said, "I'm sure it will.
I have good ideas.
And this is one of my best."

Little Pig and Big Pig went inside
to eat supper.
Then they went to sleep.

In the morning Big Pig heard—
caw, caw! Caw, caw!
He ran to the window.
He yelled, "Go away, crows!
This is not *your* house.
This is *my* house.
Can't you read the sign?"

Big Pig did not know what to do.
So he turned to Little Pig.
"Little Pig, can you help?
The crows won't listen to me."

Little Pig nodded.
"I can help," he said.
"Wait here. I'll be back soon.
I have an idea of my own."

Little Pig ran downstairs.
He found an old sheet, a broom,
a ball of string, and a marker.

Little Pig heard Big Pig calling.
"Little Pig, where are you?
What are you doing?"
Little Pig answered, "Just wait."

Big Pig waited and waited
and waited.
He got tired of waiting.
"Little Pig, where are you?" he called.

Little Pig did not answer.
But Big Pig saw something
moving in the garden.
What could it be?

A scarecrow—
Little Pig was carrying a scarecrow!
"Scarecrows *scare crows*,"
said Little Pig. "Get it?"
"I get it!" said Big Pig.

"Do you like my idea?" Little Pig asked.
"Very much," said Big Pig.
"But *I* had a better one!"
"What?" asked Little Pig.
"It was *my idea* to ask you for *your idea*!"

Little Pig said, "Look at those crows.
They are all flying away!"
Then Big Pig and Little Pig had
the best idea of all.

They decided to have a party.
A party for two.
And no crows allowed!

TRI-CITIES CHRISTIAN SCHOOLS
AIRPORT CENTER